Dedication

To all children around the world who loves to learn like this little girl, we hope you enjoy this trip to the zoo, and we wish it will be a lot of fun for you.
Thank you for learning with me.

Love Levi

Levi Enterprises LLC.

ELEPHANT

The first animal I seen was the biggest of them all, it had thick skin and was very tall.

LIONS

The second animal to see came in a pack of three.
The strong and sleepy lions didn't even look at me.

WOLF

In this enclosure another pack, a pack of wolves to see and if I listen closely, I can hear the wolves howl at me.

Reindeer

The next animal near is the pretty brown reindeer.

Kangaroo

I am so excited I love the zoo look over there a jumping Kangaroo.

Penguin

I must go into a cold enclosure to see this swimming bird.

Zebra

Outside of the enclosure I seen Zebras in a herd.

Leopard

Look up there I spotted something
with spots sleeping a lot.

Peacock

The next animal to see are the pretty colorful peacock.

Cheetah

The fastest animal in the zoo lets go look at the cheetah too.

Monkeys

What's a trip to the zoo without
seeing the swinging monkeys.

Giraffe

Over the very next wall it was so big and tall, the tallest of them all.

Silverback Gorillas

This next group hangs out in a troop, they're strong with silver backs.

Polar Bear

It would not be fair if I did not see the white and swimming polar bear.

Turtle

They usually live to be old, has a hard shell and moves slow.

Alligator

Another reptile family member will eat just about anything they can catch for dinner. The alligator moves quick and has powerful jaws with a snout shaped like a letter U.

Crocodile

Like the alligator but not quite it's the crocodile, its snout will give you more of a V bite.

Chimpanzee

What do I see hanging in the tree, it's a chimpanzee.

Tiger

The largest cat, that we can look at and it has stripped fur.

Ostrich

The largest and fastest bird of them all, the ostrich long legs and neck makes them so very tall.

Rhinoceros

The next exhibit is the rhinos spot,
the horn grows and never stops.

Camel

One last animal I want to see before its time to go, one, two, or even three humps is on this animal. Can I ride the camel ?

I had so much fun on my trip to the zoo,
I learn so much about these animals how about you ?

Made in the USA
Coppell, TX
01 September 2021